Aaron's Awful Allergies

For Ripley, Gwedhen and Sam,
the sneezers in my family — TH
For Marlys — EF

Text © 1996 Troon Harrison
Illustrations © 1996 Eugenie Fernandes

Kids Can Press acknowledges the financial support of the Ontario Arts Council, the Canada Council for the Arts and the Government of Canada, through the BPIDP, for our publishing activity.

Published in Canada by
Kids Can Press Ltd.
29 Birch Avenue
Toronto, ON M4V 1E2

Published in the U.S. by
Kids Can Press Ltd.
2250 Military Road
Tonawanda, NY 14150

www.kidscanpress.com

The artwork in this book was rendered in gouache on Arches watercolor paper.

The text is set in Joanna.

Edited by Debbie Rogosin
Designed by Marie Bartholomew
Printed in Hong Kong, China, by Wing King Tong Company Limited

The hardcover edition of this book is smyth sewn casebound.
The paperback edition of this book is limp sewn with a drawn-on cover.

CMC 96 0 9 8 7 6 5 4 3
CMC PA 98 0 9 8 7 6 5 4 3 2

Canadian Cataloguing in Publication Data

Harrison, Troon
   Aaron's awful allergies

ISBN 1-55074-299-X (bound)   ISBN 1-55074-422-4 (pbk.)

I. Fernandes, Eugenie, 1943– . II. Title.

PS8565.A66A72 1996   jC813'.54   C96-930083-2
PZ7.H36Aa 1996

Kids Can Press is a l'orus™ Entertainment company

Aaron's Awful Allergies

Story by Troon Harrison

Pictures by Eugenie Fernandes

Kids Can Press

More than anything else in the world, Aaron loved animals. He loved them more than chocolate ice cream or hockey cards or roller coasters.

Clancy was Aaron's first pet. His parents bought him for Aaron's fifth birthday. The pet-store man said Clancy would only be a small dog when he grew up. He didn't know much about puppies.

Aaron's mom thought Clancy should sleep on the mat, but Aaron liked a crowded bed.

Aaron's second pet was a calico cat that wandered
into the yard looking for a home. She soon grew fat
and contented. When she had six kittens, they slept
under Aaron's bed.

On the last day of school, Aaron volunteered to take the guinea pigs home. The teacher said that Fred and Frisky were both males.

Fred had four babies on the fifth of July.

"Teachers don't know everything," said Aaron.

Aaron loved looking after his animals. He
cleaned the guinea pig cage twice a week and
walked the dog twice a day. He played wool
games with the kittens and fed the cat.

As the summer passed, Aaron began to feel
tired. Then he felt miserable. His head ached and
his eyes were itchy and sore. Sometimes
he had a cough that made it hard to breathe.
Huge sneezes rattled his teeth.

Aaron's mom took him to the doctor.

"I think Aaron has allergies," the doctor said.

The nurse tested Aaron for allergies to dust and allergies to pollen, for allergies to milk and mold and peanut butter. Finally she tested him for allergies to animals.

"No wonder Aaron has been sneezing so much," the doctor said. "He's allergic to cats and dogs. He shouldn't play with guinea pigs or skunks—"

"Skunks!" exclaimed Aaron's mom. "We don't have any skunks!"

"And he mustn't go dancing with orangutans or leopards," said the doctor.

Aaron laughed. "We don't have any orangutans or leopards."

"Aaron is allergic to some animals," Aaron's mom told his dad that night. "We will have to find new homes for our pets."

"It's not fair!" Aaron shouted. "My animals don't want new homes. I love my animals!"

"I know this is hard for you," said his mom, "but the animals have to go."

After supper Aaron sat in his tree fort. Birds sang their evening chorus. Night animals rustled in the grass.

"At least I can still listen to the wild animals," Aaron whispered.

The kittens went to the pet store. The calico cat moved in with a lady who lived on the next block. Aaron missed the kittens' tiny meows.

Aaron's teacher took the guinea pigs. Now there was a big space on Aaron's bedroom floor. There were no more happy guinea pig squeaks.

Only Clancy was left.

"Please?" Aaron pleaded.

"No," his mom replied sadly. "Clancy has to go, too."

"Clancy is my best friend!" cried Aaron. "He keeps me warm at night and scares away the monsters under my bed. I'm allergic to monsters. Please let me keep Clancy. I don't care if I get headaches and sore eyes."

But Clancy went to live on a farm.

"This is the worst thing that's ever happened!" Aaron cried.

Aaron had nothing to take care of. Sometimes he just lay on his bed and felt sad. Sometimes he sat at the kitchen table doing nothing at all.

Aaron's mom suggested building a bird house, but Aaron didn't feel like hammering. His dad suggested painting a picture but Aaron didn't feel like painting.

"Cheer up," coaxed his mom. "Soon we'll go camping."

"I don't want to go camping," said Aaron. "And I don't want allergies. I just want my animals back."

One day Aaron found a bowl on the counter, with a fish swimming in it.

"It's for you," said his mom.

"I don't want a stupid fish," grumbled Aaron. "What good is a fish?"

One morning Aaron noticed how the fish's scales flashed in the sunlight and how its tail fluttered through the water.

"I think it's wagging its tail at me," said Aaron. "Maybe it wants to go for a walk."

After they had gone two blocks Aaron began to think it was nice to have a pet that didn't run off or chase cars or get lost.

"Hey," called Brian, "what kind of fish is that?"

"It's a shark," replied Aaron. "I call it Flash."

"Cool!" said Brian. "Trade you twenty hockey cards for it?"

"No way," answered Aaron.

That night Aaron took Flash to his bedroom. Watching
the fish swim in the moonlight made Aaron feel peaceful.

On Saturday Aaron took Flash to the movies.
It was nice not to have to share his popcorn.

Aaron made a special elevator in his tree fort so that Flash could come up.

When Aaron's family went camping,
Flash and Aaron shared a tent. They spent
their afternoons at the lake. Flash was an
excellent swimmer.

After their vacation, Aaron felt much better. He
wondered what other creatures there were to love.
And it didn't take him very long to find out.